作者／母袋裕子（Motai Hiroko）

日本童書作家。1972年出生於日本神奈川縣，現居住在東京近郊。《千千萬萬個聖誕老公公》是她出版的第一部作品。

繪者／瑪麗卡‧邁亞拉（Marika Maijala）

芬蘭獨立插畫家。1974年出生於芬蘭，學習過平面設計和電影。作品曾獲提名2019年北歐理事會兒童和青少年文學獎（The Nordic Council Children and Young People's Literature Prize），及入選2019年義大利波隆那國際童書插畫展（Bologna Illustrators Exhibition）等。

譯者／羅凡怡

曾任出版社編輯，還在半路上努力的插畫家，現職是兩個孩子的媽，最喜歡講故事給孩子聽。譯有以色列國寶級繪本《小銀魚三部曲》《小企鵝的祕密大冒險》《愛玩，愛畫，愛上繽紛大自然》《我愛泥巴》（野人出版）、《圖解野外求生聖經》（貓頭鷹出版）、《動物大百科》（木馬出版）。

小野人25

千千萬萬個聖誕老公公

中英雙語對照版

作　　者	母袋裕子（Motai Hiroko）
繪　　者	瑪麗卡‧邁亞拉（Marika Maijala）
譯　　者	羅凡怡

社　　長	張瑩瑩
總 編 輯	蔡麗真
責任編輯	陳瑾璇
行銷企劃	林麗紅
封面設計	周家瑤
美術設計	洪素貞

出　　版　野人文化股份有限公司
發　　行　遠足文化事業股份有限公司（讀書共和國出版集團）
　　　　　地址：231新北市新店區民權路108-2號9樓
　　　　　電話：（02）2218-1417　傳真：（02）8667-1065
　　　　　電子信箱：service@bookrep.com.tw
　　　　　網址：www.bookrep.com.tw
　　　　　郵撥帳號：19504465遠足文化事業股份有限公司
　　　　　客服專線：0800-221-029
法律顧問　華洋法律事務所　蘇文生律師
印　　製　成陽印刷股份有限公司
初版首刷　2019年11月
初版11刷　2023年11月

Original title: Million Billion Santa Clauses
Text © Hiroko Motai 2014
Illustrations © Marika Maijala 2014
Complex Chinese edition copyright © Yeren Publishing House, 2019
Published originally in Finnish and Swedish translations by Schildts & Söderströms.
Published by arrangement with Helsinki Literary Agency, through The Grayhawk Agency.

千千萬萬個聖誕老公公

線上讀者回函專用 QR CODE，你的寶貴意見，將是我們進步的最大動力。

野人文化
官方網頁

野人文化
讀者回函

Million Billion
Santa Clauses

千千
萬萬個
聖誕老公公

中英雙語對照版

母袋裕子 MOTAI HIROKO 著
瑪麗卡・邁亞拉 MARIKA MAIJALA 繪

很久很久以前，
世界上只有一個聖誕老公公。

A long time ago,
there was only one
Santa Claus in the world.

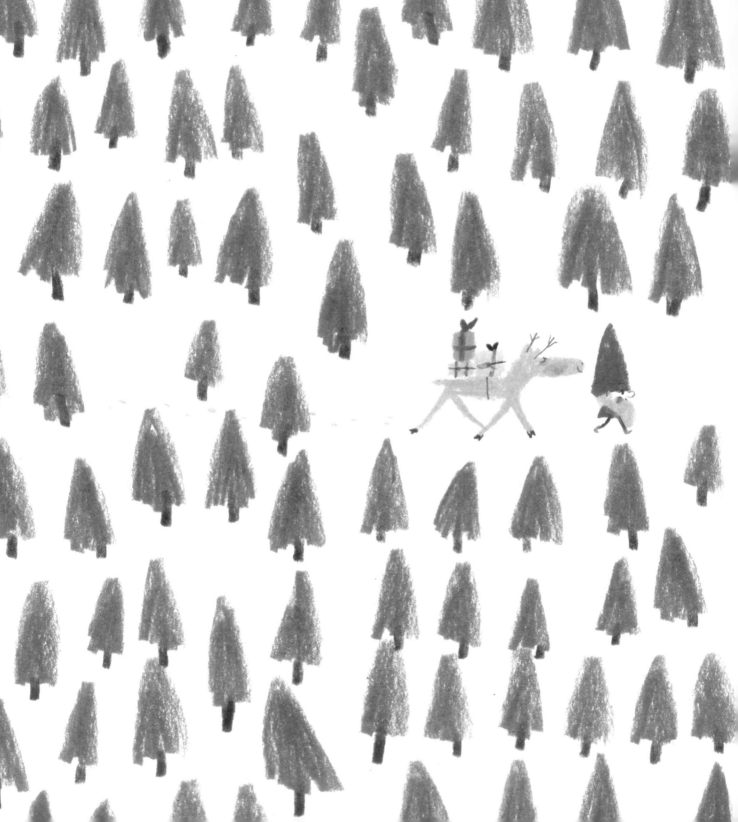

因為那個時候，世界上的人非常非常少。

Because there were very few people throughout the world.

小孩子也非常非常少，所以聖誕老公公能在
聖誕夜裡，將禮物送到每一個孩子手上。

每一個人都滿心歡迎聖誕老公公來到家中，
滿臉笑容地收下禮物。

Since there were only a few children, Santa Claus could
deliver presents to all the children during the night before Christmas.

Everyone welcomed Santa Claus into their homes and
received their presents with a smile.

這讓聖誕老公公覺得很快樂。

Santa Claus was happy.

可是慢慢地，人愈來愈多，小孩子也愈來愈多。

But gradually, the number of people grew.
The number of children grew, too.

聖誕老公公愈來愈難在一個晚上就把禮
物送到每一個小孩的手上。他時不時要
讓馴鹿休息一下，裝禮物的袋子也愈來
愈重。

It became difficult for one Santa Claus to deliver presents to all the children during just one night. He had
to let the reindeer take a rest, the present bag also
became heavier and heavier.

於是，聖誕老公公向神祈求：
「神啊！請把我變成兩個聖誕老公公吧！」

And so, Santa Claus asked God:
'God, please make me into two Santas.'

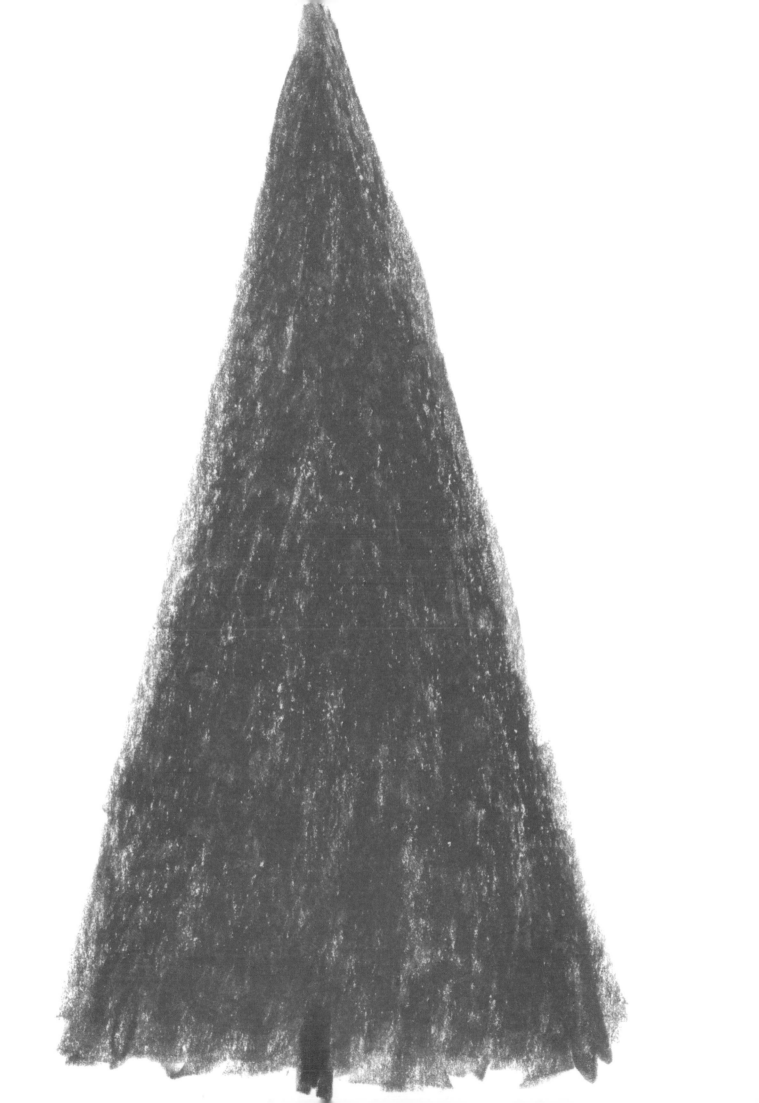

神實現了他的願望。
就這樣，一個聖誕老公公變成了兩個聖誕老公公。

God fulfilled this wish.
Then, the one Santa Claus became two Santa Clauses.

有了兩個聖誕老公公之後，
送禮物給小朋友的速度比
以前快了兩倍。這讓他們鬆
了一口氣。

Two Santa Clauses could deliver
presents to all the children twice as
fast as before. Both Santa Clauses
sighed with relief.

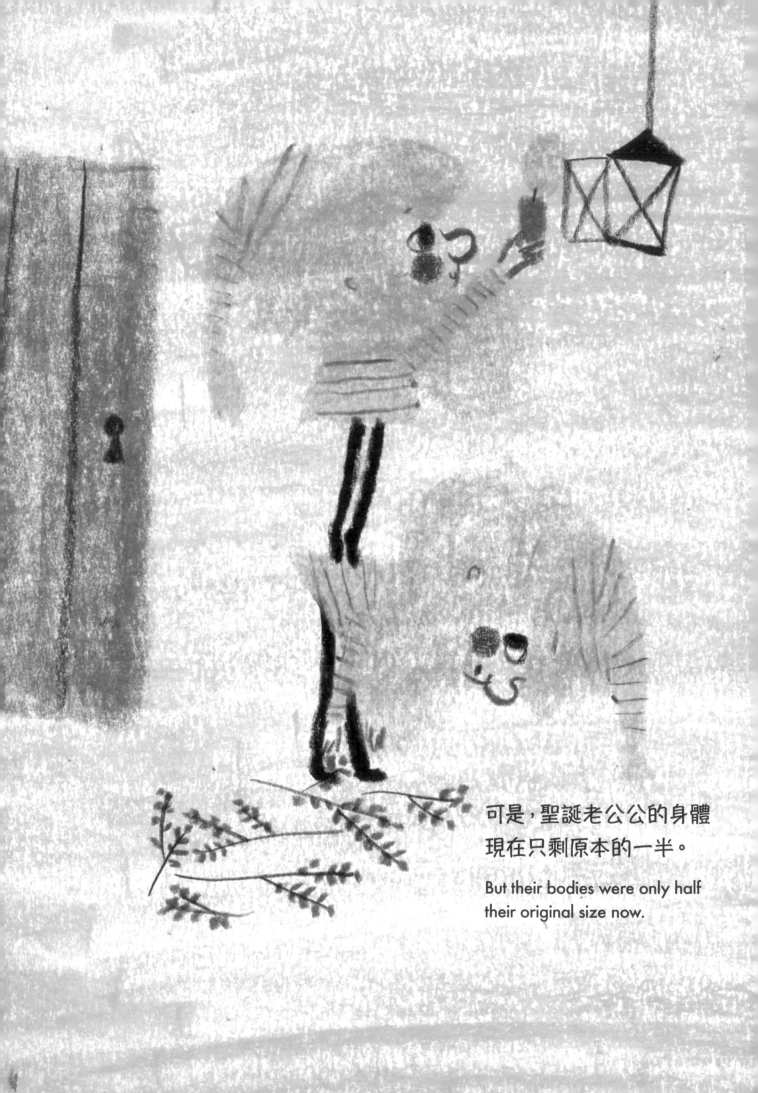

可是，聖誕老公公的身體
現在只剩原本的一半。

But their bodies were only half
their original size now.

後來，人又愈來愈多了，小孩也愈來愈多。
即使有兩個聖誕老公公，也很難在一個晚上
將禮物送到每一個孩子的手上。

In time, the number of people grew some more.

The number of children grew, too.

Even with two Santa Clauses, it became difficult
to deliver presents to all the children in just one night.

於是，兩個聖誕老公公向神祈求：
「神啊！請把我們變成四個聖誕老公公吧！」

And so, the two Santa Clauses asked God:
'God, please make us into four Santas.'

神實現了他們的願望。
就這樣，兩個聖誕老公公變成了四個聖誕老公公。

God fulfilled this wish.
Then, the two Santa Clauses became four Santa Clauses.

到了聖誕夜那一天，四位聖誕老公公把四袋禮物裝到四輛雪橇上，到世界各地送禮物給每一個孩子。

When Christmas Eve came, the four Santa Clauses loaded four sleds with four bags and delivered presents to all the children who lived throughout the world.

可是，現在他們的身體大小
只有原本的四分之一。

But their bodies were only
a fourth of their original size now.

＊從這個時候起，有一些聖誕老公公開始會
　從煙囪進到家裡，因為身體的大小剛剛好。

* Since then, a part of them started to using
chimney to enter human's house. Their little
body suited for it.

日子一天天過去，人的數量愈來愈多，小孩也愈來愈多。

As time passed, the number of people grew more and more. The number of children grew more and more, too.

就連四個聖誕老公公都搞不清楚世界上究竟有多少小孩了。

Even four Santa Clauses could not grasp how many children were in the world.

於是，四個聖誕老公公向神祈求：
「神啊！請把我們變成……」

And so, the four Santa Clauses asked God:
'God, please make us into…

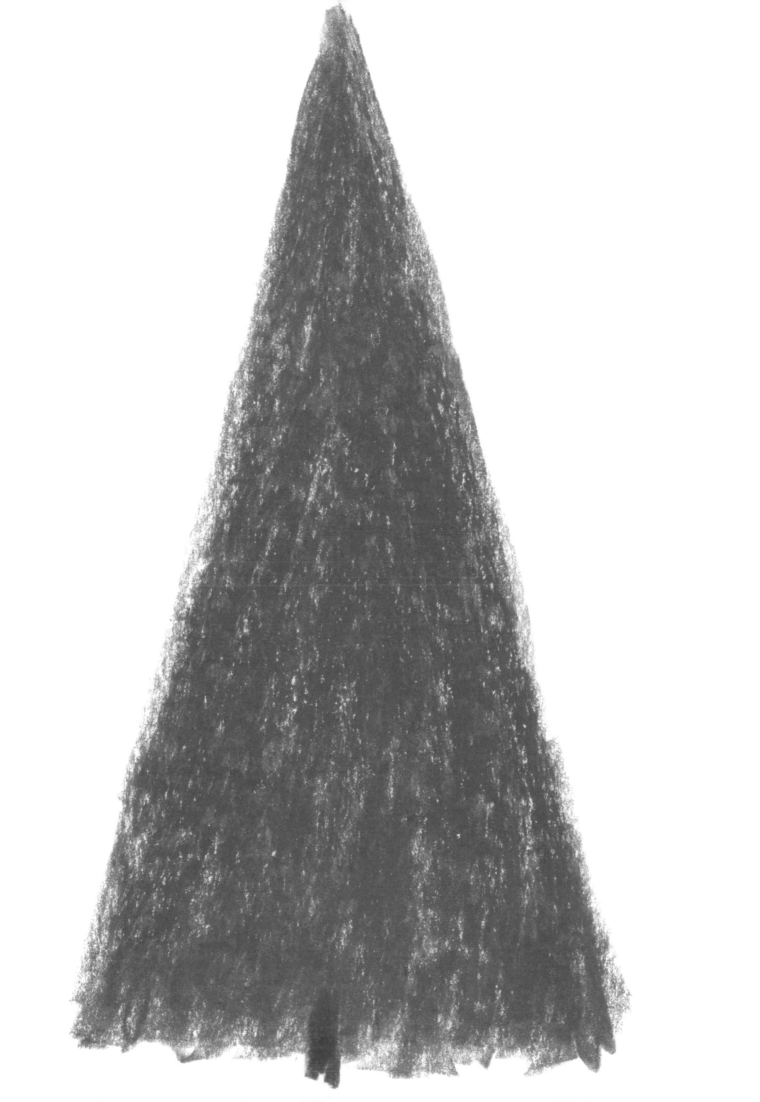

一百萬個聖誕老公公吧！」

One million Santas.'

一百萬個聖誕老公公吧！

One million Santas.'

神實現了他們的願望。
四個聖誕老公公變成一百萬個聖誕老公公。

God fulfilled this wish.
The four Santa Clauses became one million Santa Clauses.

但是，問題來了。
現在他們的身體大小只有原本的百萬分之一，
小到根本連一份禮物都拿不動。

But there was a problem.
Now, their bodies were only 1,000,000th of their original
size. They were too small to even lift up a present.

一百萬個聖誕老公公彼此商量討論該怎麼辦才好。

The one million Santa Clauses consulted one another.

然後，他們想到了一個好辦法。

Then, a good idea occurred.

那年冬天，這一百萬個聖誕老公公偷偷地
溜到一百萬個大人的耳邊，輕輕地說：

That winter, the one million Santa Clauses
slipped into the ears of one million adults
and whispered to them:

「幫每一個孩子準備一份禮物吧。」

'Give each child a present.'

一百萬個大人照做了。
雖然不確定為什麼要這麼做，他們還是為每一個孩子準備了禮物，興奮地期待聖誕節的到來。

The one million adults obeyed this order.
Though they weren't sure why, they got presents for all the children and excitedly waited for Christmas.

到了聖誕夜的那一天，一百萬個大人滿心歡喜地
把禮物藏在一百萬隻長筒襪裡。

When Christmas Eve came, they hid the presents with happy
smiles in one million stockings.

然後，時光不斷飛逝而過，人變得更多更多，
當然，聖誕老公公也變得更多更多了。
現在，他們的身體已經小到連肉眼都無法辨認了。

Then, as more and more time passed,
the number of people grew more and more.
And, of course, the number of Santa Clauses grew more and more as well.

Now, their bodies are too small to be visible to the naked eye.

再也沒有人看得見聖誕老公公了。

No one can see a Santa Claus.

可是，即使到今天，千千萬萬個聖誕老公公
還是會偷偷溜到大人的耳邊，輕輕地說：
「幫每一個孩子準備一份禮物吧！」

Yet even now, a million billion Santa Clauses are slipping
into the ears of adults and whispering to them:
'Give each child a present.'

而且我們還是繼續遵守著這個指示。

We are still obeying this order.